Stanley's Wild Ride

For Sophie — good dog, great pal and
constant inspiration — L.B.

For Spencer, who is no doubt making
a whole new batch of friends — B.S.

First paperback edition 2008

Text © 2006 Linda Bailey
Illustrations © 2006 Bill Slavin

Kids Can Press acknowledges the financial support of the Government of Ontario,
through the Ontario Media Development Corporation's Ontario Book Initiative;
the Ontario Arts Council; the Canada Council for the Arts; and the Government
of Canada, through the BPIDP, for our publishing activity.

Published in Canada by
Kids Can Press Ltd.
29 Birch Avenue
Toronto, ON M4V 1E2

Published in the U.S. by
Kids Can Press Ltd.
2250 Military Road
Tonawanda, NY 14150

www.kidscanpress.com

The artwork in this book was rendered in acrylics, on gessoed paper.
The text is set in Leawood Medium.

Edited by Debbie Rogosin
Designed by Julia Naimska
Printed and bound in China

The hardcover edition of this book is smyth sewn casebound.
The paperback edition of this book is limp sewn with a drawn-on cover.

CM 06 0 9 8 7 6 5 4 3
CM PA 08 0 9 8 7 6 5 4 3 2 1

Library and Archives Canada Cataloguing in Publication

Bailey, Linda, 1948–
Stanley's wild ride / written by Linda Bailey ; illustrated by
Bill Slavin.

ISBN 978-1-55337-960-7 (bound). ISBN 978-1-55453-254-4 (pbk.)

I. Slavin, Bill II. Title.

PS8553.A3644S74 2006   jC813'.54   C2005-904319-9

Kids Can Press is a *corus*™ Entertainment company

Stanley's Wild Ride

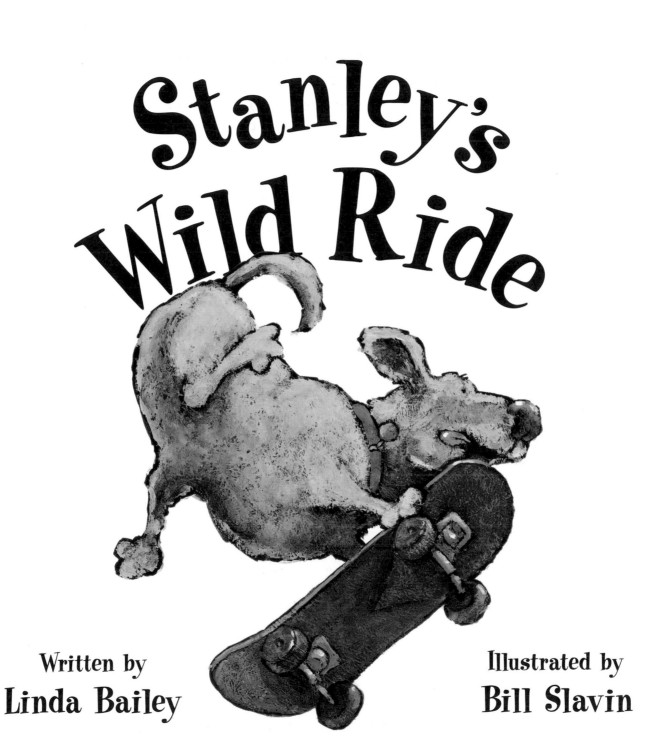

Written by
Linda Bailey

Illustrated by
Bill Slavin

KIDS CAN PRESS

Stanley knew he wasn't supposed to leave the yard.

But he'd been stuck in that yard practically his whole life. And it was always the same. Same old bush. Same old clothesline. Same old fence.

Stanley stared at the big blue sky beyond the fence, and he longed with all his heart for something new. Something exciting. Something ... MORE!

And one day, sniffing in a corner, he found it.

A hole.

Just a weensy hole, as big as a bug. But when Stanley scratched, it got bigger. Soon it was as big as a dog's nose. All afternoon and into the evening, Stanley scratched and pawed and dug.

Finally, the hole was as big as a whole dog. Stanley knew, because there he was — on the *other* side of the fence.

"Kruff!" barked Stanley in astonishment.

Then he noticed something even better. There was no leash attached to his collar. And no person at the end of the leash!

Stanley quivered with excitement. He wondered how far he could run without stopping.

He ran all the way to the end of the block.

Then he ran back.

Then he did it again!

Stanley felt like a million dog biscuits. He ran three whole blocks — without stopping! — to see his best friend, Alice.

When Alice saw Stanley running loose, she got very excited.

"Just dig a hole," said Stanley in dog talk. "It's easy."

Alice tried, but the dirt was too hard.

"There must be a way," said Stanley.

Alice poked at her fence and prodded. Finally she found a loose board that was *exactly* the size of a dog.

"Run for it!" barked Stanley, and they did.

Next came Nutsy. With Alice's help, she broke out in seconds.

Elwood's escape was tougher.

And Gassy Jack *almost* didn't make it.

But finally, there they were. Five dogs, out of their yards, and not a leash in sight!

"We can go anywhere!" barked Stanley. "We can do anything we want!"

"Yep! Yep! Yep! Yep!" agreed his friends.

And away they all ran, looking for the kind of fun you can't find in a yard. When they found some tasty garbage, they ate it. When they passed a fancy car, they soaked its tires. When they came across a tomcat, they chased it up a tree.

"And *stay* there!" growled Nutsy.

They ran all around the wild side of town. And whenever they saw a road that went up, they took it — because that night, the sky was the limit! Up the dogs went, and up and up, until finally they reached the top of the Big Hill.

With their eyes bugging out, they looked around.

"We can see the whole world from here!" cried Alice.

Stanley stared in amazement. He had no idea the world was so big.

Then he looked down. And *that's* when he saw it. Standing there in the moonlight. A strange, flat, red and black ...

Thing!

Stanley shivered. He wasn't sure what the thing was, but there was something about it that made his fur stand up. He walked slowly over and sniffed.

"Smells like feet," he said.

The other dogs crowded close and took deep sniffs. They *loved* the smell of feet.

"It's supposed to have a kid on it," said Elwood. "Where's the kid?"

The dogs all looked around. No kid.

As Stanley sniffed the thing some more, he accidentally touched it with his nose.

It moved!

He touched it again. Slowly, very slowly, it started rolling ... down ... the ... hill ...

"It's getting away!" yelped Alice.

Stanley raced after the thing. He jumped on it with all four paws to stop it.

But it didn't stop. It was going faster every second. *And it was taking Stanley with it!*

"Hot dog!" barked Nutsy. "Look at that pup go."

Stanley had never gone so fast in all his life! His ears
flew back. His fur flattened out. He held on so tight, his
paws went white!

"Go, Stanley!" yapped his friends as they raced along
behind.

Tearing around a bend, Stanley ripped
through a tunnel and over a curb. Finally,
he glanced back and saw —

His friends had found things, too!

"OW-OW-OWOOO!" howled Stanley.

Screaming into an intersection, he did a huge circling wheelie, and when he reached the top of the steepest slope in town, his friends were right on his tail!

"OW-OW-OWOOO!" they howled.

With a rumble like thunder, the dogs roared down the hill. Faster than a squirrel! Faster than a rabbit! Faster than any dog ever *dreamed* of going.

"OW-OW-OWOOO!"

And all over town, dogs woke up and howled right back. And cats yowled, and babies wailed, and lights went on, and people ran out to watch the dogs go by.

Even the *cars* were howling! There was one right behind the dogs. It was black and white and had a light on top.

"EEE-OOO! EEE-OOO!" howled the police car.

"OW-OW-OWOOO!" howled Stanley as he looked straight ahead at —

A fence!

"OW!" went the dogs as they hit the fence. "OW! OW! OW! OW!"

Well, they didn't hit it *that* hard. But it must have been a very old fence because it fell right over, and there the dogs were —

In Stanley's yard!

And there were Stanley's people on the porch, wearing their pajamas. Stanley went over to give them a lick. They tasted sleepy.

It took a while to sort everything out. Stanley's friends were loaded into the police car to go home. The things with wheels went into the trunk.